CROCODILE, YOU'RE Beautiful

Embracing Our Strengths and Ourselves

By Dr. Ruth K. Westheimer and Dena Neusner • Illustrated by CB Decker
Parent note by Ruth K. Westheimer with Pierre Lehu

For my four grandchildren, Ari, Leora, Michal, and Ben, who were the inspiration for this book
and who inspire me every day with their talents, family values, and love for their Omi.
— RKW

For my mother, who taught me to be true to myself, with love.
— DN

To Rutherford McGee, a young illustrator who inspires me.
— CBD

For my three grandchildren, Jude, Rhys, and Isabelle.
— PL

Editorial consultants: Dr. Halana Rothbort and Dvorah Levy, LCWS

Apples & Honey Press
An Imprint of Behrman House Publishers
Millburn, New Jersey 07041
www.applesandhoneypress.com

Text copyright ©2019 Behrman House Publisher
Art copyright ©2019 by CB Decker
ISBN 978-1-68115-551-7

Library of Congress Cataloging-in-Publication Data

Names: Westheimer, Ruth K. (Ruth Karola), 1928- author. | Neusner, Dena, author. | Lehu, Pierre A., author. | Decker, C. B., illustrator.
Title: Crocodile, you're beautiful! : embracing our strengths and ourselves / by Dr. Ruth K. Westheimer, Dena Neusner, and Pierre A. Lehu ; illustrated by CB Decker.
Other titles: Crocodile, you are beautiful!
Description: Millburn NJ : Apples & Honey Press, 2019. | Summary: Dr. Ruth Westheimer meets an assortment of animals and spreads the message that everyone has a different body and each body has its own strengths.
Identifiers: LCCN 2018037182 | ISBN 9781681155517 (alk. paper)
Subjects: | CYAC: Animals--Fiction. | Self-acceptance--Fiction. | Individuality--Fiction.
Classification: LCC PZ7.1.W4375 Cr 2019 | DDC [E]--dc23 LC record available at https://lccn.loc.gov/2018037182

All rights reserved. No part of this publication may be translated, reproduced, stored in a retrieval system or transmitted in any form or by any means, electronic, mechanical, photocopying, recording or otherwise without express written permission from the publishers.

Edited and art directed by Ann D. Koffsky
Design by Alexandra N. Segal

Printed in the United States of America
1 3 5 7 9 8 6 4 2

I have a body. You have a body.
Each of us has eyes for seeing.
We have hands for touching.
We have arms for reaching
. . . or wings for flapping!

But your body is different from mine.
Why? Because it's all yours.
Only you can make your body move.
You are in charge of your body.
But sometimes this is hard . . .

Try This!

Move all the parts of your body at once.
Ready, set, go!

Try This!

Stand up tall, stretch out your arms, and say,
"This is my space."

Try This!

Look at yourself in the mirror.
Say to yourself,
"My body is just right for me."

I think Cat has something to say.

Try This!

With a friend, practice saying no
without being mean.
Try using different words
and voices too.

...with a carrot chip cookie for dessert. Yum!

Try This!

Have an "everyone is different" party! With some friends, make a list of all the ways you are different from each other.

Try This!

Think of something you're good at.
Draw yourself doing it while
wearing a superhero cape!

Try This!

Jump up and down. Do some jumping jacks. Then stand tall and make muscles with your arms.
Feel the strength in your body.

Whether you're an octopus or a crocodile, a cat, a rabbit, a turtle, or an ant — or even a human! — your body is just right for you.

You are in charge of your body.

Try This!

Say it out loud with me:
"I'm in charge of my body!
My body is just right for me!"

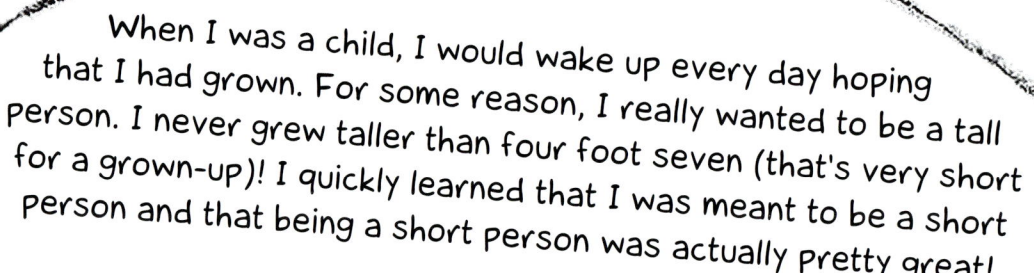

When I was a child, I would wake up every day hoping that I had grown. For some reason, I really wanted to be a tall person. I never grew taller than four foot seven (that's very short for a grown-up)! I quickly learned that I was meant to be a short person and that being a short person was actually pretty great!

Did anyone ever make fun of me for being short? Of course. That's how I learned how important it is never to make fun of the shape or size of anyone's body. Everybody, and every **body**, deserves respect.

Because this meant so much to me, I decided that when I grew up, I'd become an expert at helping people understand that we are each in charge of our own body.

And I did!

In this book, I help lots of animals understand this as well. You can talk about it with your family too:

- Have you ever felt like one of the animals in this book? Which one?
- Ant is strong at building, and Turtle is strong at swimming. What are you strong at?
- Have your friends ever wanted you to try something that just wasn't right for you, as Rabbit's friends did? What happened?

Learn to discover who you are and what makes you happy. Then pat yourself on the back.

You deserve it!